How The
UNICORN
Was Born

This book belongs to:

For my family.

How The UNICORN Was Born

Written by

Charlotte Daniels

Illustrated by

Hannah Marks

There once was a foal

With a horn on her head.

She was born to be different,
Her proud mother said.

But a grumpy bull lived
In the next field along.
And he tried to say
That the foal's horn was wrong!

"It's bulls that have horns,"
Said the bull, being mean.
"I'd say that this foal
Is like no one I've seen."

When the mare heard these words,
Her reaction was swift.

She said, "We all are unique,
With our own special gift."

Now, it happened that there
Was a duck on the farm,
Who just didn't share
The bull's sense of alarm.

She said to her ducklings,
"Ignore all of Bull's chatter.
You can play with the foal—
Being different won't matter."

First the foal showed the ducklings
How fast she could run.

Then the ducklings showed foal
All their pond diving fun.

And as the foal slept
Under stars and moonbeams,
She flew with the ducks
In her wildest dreams.

Now the foal had made friends,
So, as the time passed,
The mean words from Bull
Seemed forgotten at last.

And, in Foal's heart, grew a wish
That one day she might share
The sky with the ducks,
If she flew through the air.

But one dreadful day,
As Foal played with a duck,
Her horn scratched his wing—
It was terrible luck.

Yet before Foal could say
Even one sorry word,

The bull cleared his throat,
So that he could be heard.

He called out to the duck,
"It can't make you glad,

"That you have made friends
With a foal who is bad!"

The young duck called straight back,
"Yes, the foal is my friend.
She's already forgiven,
And my wing will soon mend."

Still, the day after that,
The foal grew quite sad,
And she started to think
Of a question she had.

She said, "Why must I have
A silly horn on my head,
When I'd much rather be
Simply normal instead?"

When the mare saw Foal's tears,
She said, "You will always belong.
You have made a mistake,
But being different's not wrong.

"And that horn on your head
Will have helped you to know
When you learn from mistakes,
It's a way you can grow!"

Now, the foal she was growing
In more than one way,
And, as spring turned to summer,
She had something to say.

She said, "I am a horse
With a unique horn.

I shall name myself now,
As a Unicorn!"

But when the bull heard,
He said, "You're not unique.
And you cannot change
From the words that you speak!"

The unicorn sighed,
And she gave a small frown.
She was tired of the bull
Always putting her down.

She said, "I'll be true to my word—
You watch me try.

"With the power of my mind,
Why, you'll see me fly!"

Well, the bull roared with laughter
When he heard that.

"If there's a horse that can fly,
Oh, I'll eat my hat."

So, the unicorn tried,
And each year she grew older.

And each time she failed,

Her thoughts became bolder.

HOW TO BUILD A PLANE

She worked with such focus,
And she thought with her brain.
She used her ideas,
Till she fashioned a plane.

And the animals helped her
To get the job done,
With building and painting,
With fixing things on.

Then one day when she soared
High up in the sky,
The animals looked,
And they cried, "She can fly!

"She did what she said,
She tried, failed and grew.
She used her best thoughts—
Now her dreams have come true."

But when the unicorn landed
And climbed from her seat,
The bull tried to say
It was some kind of cheat.

WELL DONE!

He said, "Gosh can't you see?
Please, let me explain.
You still cannot fly,
You're just a horse in a plane!"

But Unicorn didn't mind,
Unicorn, she was ready.

She knew what to say,
And she kept her voice steady.

She said, "Bull, you're being unfair,
Just like every day,

"So, I choose to ignore
Any words that you say!

"And I'll give you my words—
We all are unique.
You can choose your own thoughts
For the dream that you seek.

"You can pick yourself up,
You can cry, learn and laugh.

"With the use of your thoughts,
You can make your own path."

When the words, they were out,
And the thoughts were complete,
Unicorn had achieved
An astonishing feat!

For the power in her words
Made her heart shine so bright,
That she found her own magic,
In her search to take flight.

And that's how she grew wings
To reach for the sky,

So she knew in that moment,
Unicorn, she could...

FLY!

A Message From the Author:

I wrote this story because I love unicorns.
But I also wanted Foal to show some determination in the story, so she had to make a lot of non-magical choices, before she found her 'unicorn magic'. Some of the non-magical choices she made were:
- Choosing a 'real world' way to achieve what she wanted, instead of wishing for something impossible.
- Choosing to learn from other people and accept help and guidance.
- Choosing to learn from her mistakes and keep trying to learn new skills.
- Choosing to believe in herself.

Whilst humans can't use magic, I hope that Foal's non-magical choices provided some encouragement, that we too can make good choices for ourselves.

Best wishes,

Charlotte

About the Illustrator:

Hannah Marks is a self-taught illustrator and designer. She worked as a graphic designer before moving into illustration, and works digitally utilising textures to add an organic feel to her art.

You can find Hannah Marks at:

www.hannahmarks.uk

All about unicorns and other mythical horses:

Foal is slightly different to other unicorns because she names herself 'Unicorn' by putting together the words 'unique' and 'horn'. So she uses the name Unicorn all the way through the rest of the story.

In real life, people often use different names for mythical horses with horns and wings, instead of calling them a unicorn.

The word 'unicorn' comes from an old language called Latin and the meaning of the word is 'one horn.' A long time ago, people often used 'unicorn' to mean a mythical horse that didn't fly but had a horn on its head. Whereas, they called mythical horses that had wings but no horn by the name 'pegasus'.

Unicorns have also been shown in stories as being able to fly, with or without wings. Winged unicorns are often referred to as 'alicorns' or 'pegacorns', but some people also say 'winged unicorn.'

Leaving a review:

If you enjoyed this story, then the best place to leave your thoughts is in a review. They take a few minutes to write, but are always helpful and always appreciated by authors and illustrators alike. Most of all, they let other people know about the book from a reader's point of view.

Printed in Great Britain
by Amazon